# King Josh
## and his
## Amazing
## Umbrella

written by Cynthia Benjamin
illustrated by Jared Lee

**Macmillan
McGraw-Hill**

New York  Farmington

One cloudy morning, Josh got ready for school.

His raincoat was bright yellow.

His rain boots were shiny black.

And his umbrella was sky blue.

"This umbrella looks silly," Josh said.

"Why that's an umbrella fit for a king!" his mother answered.

Then she kissed him good-bye.

Josh walked along the street.

He held his umbrella up high over his head.

"Make way for King Josh!" he cried.

King Josh had a bright yellow cape.

He had shiny black boots.

And the umbrella he carried was amazing.

King Josh walked through the Dark
Woods.

On his way, he met a mighty
monster.

The monster was very, very fat and
very, very mean.

King Josh wasn't afraid.

He had his amazing umbrella.

"Take that, mighty monster!" he said.

Up went the monster.

Up, up and away.

Then King Josh walked on.

Next he met a river monster.

The river monster roared.

But King Josh wasn't afraid.

He had his amazing umbrella.

"Let the King pass!" he cried.

King Josh flew right over that
monster.

And he walked on.

Next he met a furry monster.

The furry monster was looking for food.

King Josh reached into his amazing umbrella.

He pulled out some peanuts.

"Away, furry monster!" he cried.

Whoosh!

Down the tree came the furry monster.

It grabbed the peanuts.

Then it ran away, deep into the Dark Woods.

"Ha!" said King Josh.

"All the monsters have fallen!"

And he walked on.

Finally King Josh got to school.

"Make way for the King!" he said.

He took off his bright yellow cape and his shiny black boots.

He put away his sky-blue umbrella.

Then King Josh was just Josh again.

But when it was time to go home to
the Castle, he became King Josh again.